P9-CRZ-410

To Brian, who puts the pop in my wheelie.

DIAL BOOKS FOR YOUNG READERS · Penguin Young Readers Group
An imprint of Penguin Random House LLC · 375 Hudson Street, New York, New York 10014

ISBN 9780399186653
Printed in China · 10 9 8 7 6 5 4 3 2 1
Designed by Jason Henry · Text set in Gotham and Hank BT
The artwork for this book was created with acrylic paint on Bristol board.

Friends Stick Together

Hannah E. Harrison

Dial Books for Young Readers

sym•bi•o•sis \ˌsim-bē-ˈō-səs, -ˌbī\ *n*

1: a close association of animals or plants of a different species that is often, but not always, of mutual benefit

I’m Rupert.

I like reading
dictionaries,

listening to
classical overtures,

and eating cucumber
sandwiches with no crust.

This is Levi.
He's a tickbird.

He likes corny jokes,

"Why do bees always have sticky hair?
Because they use HONEYCOMBS!
HA HA HA HA!"

PFFT!
POOT!
PFFFFFT!

armpit farts,

and popping wheelies.

He just showed up one day,

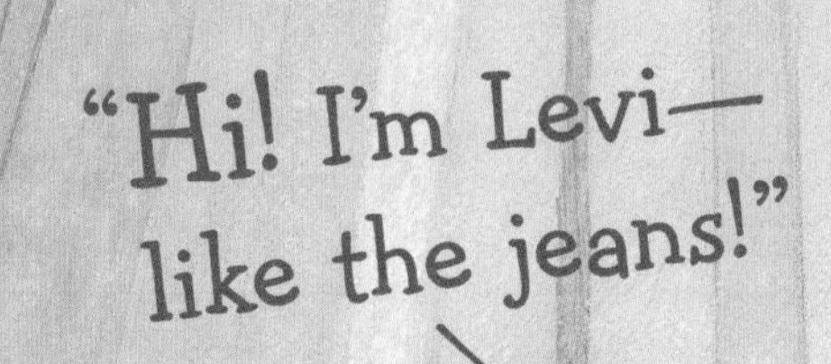

and sat on my nose,

and now I'm stuck with him.

The other birds are cool.

Harold recites Shakespeare.

"To be or not to be, that is the question."

Judith can sing opera.

"Figaro! Figaro! Fiiiig-a-rooow!"

But Levi?
Levi burps the alphabet.

Making friends was hard before.

But now, it's pretty much impossible.

In music class, Levi likes to play “epic” air guitar solos at inappropriate times.

During lunch, he makes a big to-do about eating my ticks, and grosses everyone out.

And in gym class,
he draws even
more attention to
my shameful lack of
upper body strength.

"No worries, Rupie!
I'll be the brawn,
you be the brains!"

Levi has **got** to go.

TWOOT!!!!
TWOOT!!
TWOOT!!!
TWOOT!!
TWOOT!!
TWOOT!
TWOOT!
TWOOT!
TWOOT!
TWOOT!
TWOOT!
TWOOT!

So in music class I play wrong notes
loudly in Levi's direction.

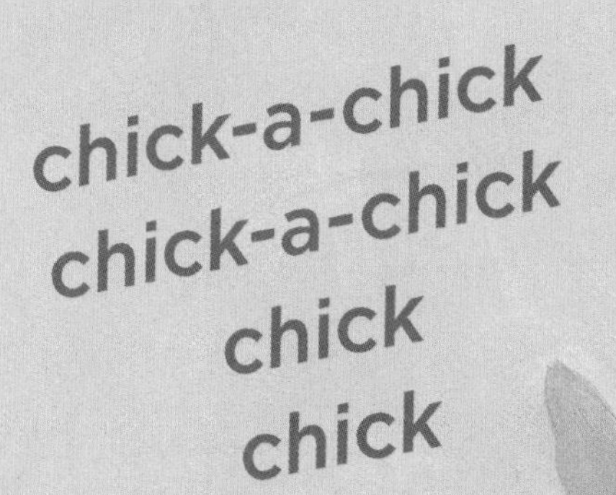

BE-DO-DO
BE-DO-DO
BEE BEE
BOOOO
BOW
BA
BOW
BOW!

ting-itty
ting
ting-itty
ting

plink-itty plink-itty
plink plink

ching-a
ching-a

But he doesn't miss a beat.

During dodgeball, I twist and turn
so that Levi gets nailed by the ball

every

single

time.

But . . .

he always bounces back.

And at recess, I try flinging him off of me with centrifugal force.

I get sick in the trash can,
but Levi has the ride of his life.

I decide it's time to be direct, so I say, "Levi, I find your boisterousness a tad loathsome."

"Huh?"

"Your uncouthness is slightly problematic."

"My what?"

"I want to be alone."

"Oh,"
he says, and hops down.

"Sorry, Rupert. I just thought you looked like you could use a friend."

Then he shuffles off to go hide in a bush.

The next day at school,
Levi is nowhere to be found.

Music class is nice and harmonious. . .
but also a little boring.
plink
chick
twoot
ting
"Figaro! Figaro!
Fiiiig-a-rooow!"

At lunch, I have my favorite—
cucumber sandwiches . . .

but I can't even enjoy them
because I'm so itchy.

And in gym, instead of me *and* Levi
getting picked last for teams . . .

it's just me.

friend \'frend\ *n*

1: a person attached to another by feelings of affection

2: a person who gives assistance; a patron; supporter

3: a person who is on good terms with another; not hostile

I think Levi might have been right,

and I feel terrible.

So, after school, I go to Levi's house and knock on his door.

Knock-knock!

"Who's there?"

"Rhino."

"Rhino who?"

"Rhino I was wrong
and you were right,
and I'm really sorry.
Can we be friends?"

Levi laughs and opens the door. He says,
"I don't know—you can be a little highfalutin."

"Huh?"

"It's an adjective. Means *too big for your britches.*"

"My what?"

"Yeah," he says.
"We can be friends."

I'm Rupert.

Turns out I like *classical* air guitar, corny jokes, and my good friend, Levi.

Pling-a
Pling-a
Pling-Pling

Bee-DO-DO
Bee-DO-DO
Bee Bee

---

sym•bi•o•sis \ˌsim-bē-ˈō-səs, -ˌbī\ *n*

2: the relationship between two different kinds of living things that live together and depend on each other.